MIRIAM
in the DESERT

To my Empty Nesters Shabbat Dinner Group—J.J.

To Greta and Sergio with love—N.U.

MIRIAM
in the DESERT

by **Jacqueline Jules**

illustrated by **Natascia Ugliano**

KAR-BEN
PUBLISHING

"I'm thirsty!" a woman groans.

"In Egypt, we had water," a man grumbles.

We are Israelites. After crossing the sea and escaping Pharaoh's armies, we are wandering in the desert with Moses as our leader. There are so many people and animals that I can't see the end of the line or the beginning. But I can see my grandmother, Miriam. Like a butterfly visiting flowers, she weaves in and out, comforting everyone.

"God did not free us from slavery in Egypt to let us die of thirst," Miriam assures them. She points to a pillar of clouds billowing in the sky. By night, the cloud turns to fire. It is always with us, leading the way.

"The cloud makes me feel safe," I tell Miriam.

"God is protecting us, Bezalel," she answers.

My throat feels as if it is lined with sand. I pick up a stone to draw clouds and raindrops in the parched earth.

Finally, we arrive at a place called Marah. There is
a spring, but the water is bitter.
"Give us something we can drink!" the people demand.
Moses picks up a piece of wood and drops it into the water.
One of the men takes a sip. "Now it's sweet!"

Miriam raises her tambourine.
The women join her, singing and dancing.

Miracles, miracles
Praise God's might!
We see miracles
Day and night.

I watch their scarves swirl in circles, remembering how my grandmother led the celebration after we crossed the sea on dry land.

We leave Marah and trudge on. The wilderness is barren, with rocks and sand in all directions.

"Where are we going?" I ask Miriam. People say she is a prophetess, a wise woman who sees God's plan.

"To Canaan," she answers, "where our people will live in freedom."

The journey goes on. More rocks. More sand. More complaining.

"We're hungry!" a woman shouts.

"When we were slaves, we had food!" a man joins in.

My stomach rumbles. I pick up a stick and draw some grapes in the sand.

"We will eat soon," Miriam promises.

The next day, when we wake, something
glistens on the ground. It looks like shining pearls.
"Taste it." My grandmother smiles.
"It tastes like bread!" I say.
"To me it tastes like honey," Miriam says.
"The flavor is special in each person's mouth."
Once again she raises her tambourine.

Miracles, miracles
Praise God's might!
We see miracles
Day and night.

We are no longer hungry or thirsty when we travel. In the morning, we gather the miraculous food called manna. And at night, when we camp, a rock spouts a fountain of water. We call it Miriam's Well, in honor of my grandmother.

But the grumbling goes on and on.

"It's hot," a man complains.

"This journey is endless," a woman whines.

"When will they trust in God?" I ask my grandmother.

"Soon," she says. "We must be patient."

The pillar of clouds leads us on through the desert. Whenever I can, I walk beside Miriam. And whenever we stop, I draw pictures in the sand.

"Bezalel," my grandmother says. "God has made you an artist."

On the third new moon, we reach the foot of a mountain called Sinai.

"Get ready," Moses tells us. "Purify yourselves. Put on clean clothes."

Three days later, I wake to thunder and lightning. Miriam takes my hand, and we follow Moses to the foot of the mountain. Smoke billows amid giant flames.

The mountain shudders and shakes. A shofar sounds, growing louder and louder. Even my toes tremble.

Then just as I think my ears will burst, everything grows still. Not one baby cries. Not one sheep bleats. The earth feels as if even the worms below have stopped wiggling.

We hear a voice that comes from the east, the west, the north, the south, above, below—everywhere at once. I feel as if I am being lifted off the ground.

I am the Lord your God who brought you out of the land of Egypt, out of the house of slavery. "Everything God commands, we will do," we promise together.

That night, everyone talks about the voice at the mountain.

"It was so strong!" one man says.

"It whispered to me," a woman says.

"God spoke to each one of us in the way we understood best," Miriam explains.

The next day, Moses climbs the cloud-covered mountain. God has called him up while we have been instructed to wait. "Moses will bring us two stone tablets," Miriam tells me. "They will contain God's laws."

"They will be holy," I whisper. "We will need to place them in something safe and beautiful."

My grandmother puts her arm around me. "Something made by an artist."

"Me?" I ask in surprise.

"Yes, Bezalel," she answers. "God has chosen you to build an Ark for the Ten Commandments."

In my grandmother's eyes, I see the future. Everyone is bringing gifts and working together to build a place where we will worship God.

And Miriam is dancing with her tambourine.

Miracles, miracles
Praise God's might!
We see miracles
Day and night.

AUTHOR'S NOTE:

The Bible does not give us many details about Moses' sister Miriam. She is called a prophetess (*Exodus* 15:20), and the literature suggests that she was a leader among the Israelite women. After crossing the sea to freedom, she leads the women in dance as they rejoice in the Song of the Sea. In this story, I imagine her continuing to sing God's praises as she witnesses the many miracles in the desert.

According to legend, a sieve-like rock, spouting a fountain of water, accompanied the Israelites as they journeyed through the desert. Called Miriam's Well, it was given to the people as a reward for Miriam's devotion to God.

Bezalel, the artist chosen by God to build the Holy Ark, is said to be her descendant. Louis Ginzberg (*Legends of the Bible*) identifies him as her grandson, the relationship I have chosen for this story. According to the Talmud, *Sanhedrin* (69b), he was thirteen when God chose him as the artist to build the Ark for the Ten Commandments.

For my sources, I consulted: *Biblical Images: Men and Women of the Book* by Adin Steinsaltz, *Biblical Literacy* by Joseph Telushkin, *The Classic Tales* by Ellen Frankel, *Etz Hayim: Torah and Commentary* edited by David L. Leiber, *The Five Books of Miriam* by Ellen Frankel, *Legends of the Bible* by Louis Ginzberg, *Pentateuch and Haftorahs*, edited by J.H. Hertz, and *Sefer Ha-Aggadah: The Book of Legends for Young Readers* by Seymour Rossel.

Text copyright © 2010 by Jacqueline Jules
Illustrations © 2010 Lerner Publishing Group, Inc.

KAR-BEN PUBLISHING
A division of Lerner Publishing Group, Inc.
241 First Avenue North
Minneapolis, MN 55401 U.S.A.
1-800-4KARBEN

Website address: www.karben.com

Library of Congress Cataloging-in-Publication Data

Jules, Jacqueline, 1956–
    Miriam in the desert / by Jacqueline Jules ; illustrated by Natascia Ugliano.
        p.   cm.
    ISBN 978–0–7613–4494–0 (lib. bdg. : alk. paper)
    1. Miriam (Biblical figure)—Juvenile literature. 2. Moses (Biblical leader)
—Juvenile literature. 3. Bible stories, English—O.T. Exodus. I. Ugliano, Natascia.
II. Title.

BS580.M54J85 2010
222'.1209505—dc22
                                                2009001874

Manufactured in the United States of America
    1 – DP – 7/15/10

$8.95 U.S.A.

KARBEN
PUBLISHING
www.karben.com
800-4KARBEN